The DREAM TRAVELER'S QUEST

-4-
THE FINAL JUDGMENT

TED DEKKER
KARA DEKKER

ISBN 978-0-9968124-9-8

Theo glanced up at the clock, knees bouncing under his desk. Three more minutes. His mind clawed through clouds of worry and confusion, knowing that Annelee and Danny had to be in the same state of anxiety. They'd had to sit through their classes pretending other earth wasn't about to fall to pieces around them.

Asher had taken *The Book of History* and had vanished. They hadn't heard or seen him since he ran from the library with a Shataiki clinging to his back.

The bell finally rang. Their substitute history teacher yelled last-minute homework instructions as the students raced for the door. Theo quickly exited the room. Annelee and Danny followed. They hurried to a quiet spot behind the stairs where some old lockers had been tucked away for storage.

"We have to do something," Annelee said, pacing.

Danny collapsed against the lockers that lined the wall. "But what?"

"I don't know." She nibbled on her painted fingernail. "I just know I'll explode if we sit here doing nothing."

Danny faced Theo. "Any thoughts?"

Theo focused on his breathing, aware of the sweat rolling down his forehead. What could he do? He saw himself as their leader, the first to go to the other world, but he was clueless.

He took a deep breath. "Maybe . . ." It was as far as he got. What he was thinking seemed way too dangerous. They'd never go for it.

"What?" Annelee pressed.

"Maybe we sneak over to Asher's house tonight and see if the book is there."

She stared for a moment, considering. "My parents won't let me go out past dark."

"Neither will my dad. So, we sneak out." Theo balled his hands into fists. "I know it's a terrible idea, but if Asher finds a way to cross over and get to other earth with the Shataiki, then—"

"I know." She sighed and then lifted her hands in surrender. "Fine. I'm in."

"You're in?"

"I'm in. There's no telling what will happen if Asher crosses over."

Theo blinked, thinking his idea really was a terrible idea. He'd never deliberately undermined his dad's authority. But what choice did they have?

He nodded. "Let's meet at my house around ten; my dad should be asleep and my house is closest to Asher's."

"No invitation for the blind kid. I get it," Danny said and then forced a smile.

Annelee and Theo looked at Danny and then back at each other.

"Don't be silly," Danny said. "I would only slow you down. But promise you won't forget me if you cross over."

"Promise," Theo and Annelee said in unison.

Theo exhaled, blowing his hair off his forehead. "Let's meet at my house around ten. Dad should be asleep by then."

"That will work," Annelee said. "I think I'm only a block away from you. My bus passes your house every day."

"Theo?"

Theo turned around to find his dad, hands on hips, staring at him curiously. Had he heard them?

"Hi, Dad." He nodded at Annelee. "This is Annelee White—"

"Right! I have your sister this year."

Danny extended his hand out in front of his body before Annelee could respond. "I'm Danny!"

Theo's dad took his hand and shook it. "I know who you are. That's a firm grip you've got there, Danny." He glanced at his watch and then looked back at Theo. "You ready to go home?"

"Uh, yeah."

"Alright. Well, let's roll out. Got to get home. Papers to grade, lessons to plan."

"See you at ten," Annelee whispered. Her voice was shaky and tight. She was as nervous as Theo.

He forced a smile and followed his dad out of the school. Fear crept back into his mind. He could feel the blood draining from his face as he plopped himself in the passenger seat of the car. What if he got caught sneaking out? What if they couldn't get the book? What if Asher crossed over? Under the control of the Shataiki, there was no telling what havoc the bully could cause in other earth.

He inhaled slowly and then exhaled. He had three of the five seals. Why was he allowing fear to affect him like this?

Then he suddenly remembered what Talya had told him. The seals could be lost. Could he have lost them sometime during the day? Maybe when Asher took the book? He didn't remember feeling anything strange. Or maybe they'd disappear if he couldn't get the book back!

"Seatbelt?" his dad asked.

"Huh?"

"Did you buckle?"

Theo glanced down. He'd forgotten. He quickly pulled the belt across his lap, clicked it in place, and continued staring out the window.

"You alright?"

Theo looked at his dad. "What?" Then he glanced out the window. "Yeah, I'm fine."

"Hard day at school?"

"Something like that."

"How about some tunes? That usually cheers you up." His dad turned on the radio, allowing Queen's "We Are the Champions" to flow through the car as they cruised home.

Theo knew there was nothing he could do until later that night, so he tried to calm his racing heart, quiet his mind, and listen to his dad's favorite band. But all he could think about was Asher.

When they got home, his dad ordered a pizza. They sat on the couch watching an episode of *American Idol* recorded earlier in the week. It was a typical Thursday night—usually his favorite night.

But tonight he wasn't paying attention, nor was he hungry. Fortunately, his dad had a mound of grading to distract him.

Theo said his goodnights around nine, told his dad he was going to do some comic-book reading till he got tired, and then headed up the stairs and closed himself in.

He leaned against the door and took a deep breath. Staring around his room now, the idea of sneaking out seemed even crazier than when the thought had first jumped in his mind, but he was now committed. Annelee would be at his window soon.

"I have to," he mumbled. "No choice."

He walked over to his dresser and took out a black hooded sweatshirt and a pair of black jeans. For the first time, he realized how much of his clothing was black. He shrugged. Black helped him blend in.

He slipped on the clothes and went to his closet to pull down a box marked "winter." He rifled through the box, removed a black beanie, and placed it on his head. If he was going to sneak out and break into Asher's house, he had to melt into the night.

Break into Asher's house?

Is that what he really planned to do? He hadn't thought that far ahead. Sneaking out was one thing.

Breaking in was at a whole other level. But it's what they'd have to do to get the book. They'd probably get busted before setting a foot on Asher's lawn.

Still, they had to try.

Satisfied by the image of black in his mirror, he sat on his bed and glanced at his alarm clock: 9:25. Thirty more minutes to wait. He plopped on the bed, consumed by the questions running through his mind.

What was happening on other earth? Were the Roush okay? What was Talya going to say to him about losing the book? Was he disappointed in him? Was Elyon disappointed in him? What would happen if Shadow Man got the book?

It was too much to think about.

They had to get the book, no matter the cost.

But if they couldn't, there would be a problem, and of that he had no doubt.

His thoughts were abruptly interrupted by the sound of something striking his window. Startled, he sprang from his bed, heart hammering. Another something hit the window.

Annelee!

Theo crossed the room in four leaping strides and peered down at Annelee looking up at him from the yard below.

He glanced at his clock: 9:35. She was early.

Theo held up a finger and mouthed, *Wait there.* It was now or never.

He hurried to his door, opened it as quietly as possible, slipped out, and slowly pulled it closed behind him. So far so good. He could see the glow of light from under his dad's bedroom door. He'd moved to the bedroom.

Theo tiptoed down the stairs and exited the house through the back door. Annelee stood by the wall, dressed in all black, hair braided in pigtails. The black paint on her face made him wonder if he should have done the same thing.

"I hate this!" Annelee whispered. "And I know I'm early, but I found my opening and took it while I could. If my parents find me gone, they're going to ground me forever!"

"Then let's be quick," Theo said. "We just have to see if Asher has the book, figure out a way to grab it, and then we can head home. Easy."

Annelee stared at him

"Okay, maybe not easy, but the sooner we get back, the better." He walked past her. "Follow me."

Annelee kept right behind him as he raced across the neighborhood, keeping to the shadows. They jogged four blocks before he slowed down to catch his breath, eyes on a big white house on the corner.

He pulled up and pointed. "There."

Annelee stared, breathless. "How do you even know where he lives?"

"There was a teachers' meeting here once. I had to go with my dad. Let's just say, it wasn't a great night."

"Do you know where Asher's room is by any chance?"

"I can guess well enough."

"Guess?"

He pointed to a window on the first floor. Crudely painted signs—a skull and crossed bones and the words "Beware of Rabid Dog"—decorated the glass.

Annelee bit her lip nervously. "Good guess."

Theo held in his laugh as they slipped across the yard. They ducked under the windows and inched over to Asher's room.

"Stay down. I'll look inside," he whispered.

She nodded. She was even prettier in the moonlight.

He stood and peered into the dimly lit room. There, on the bed with the book wide open, lay Asher, seemingly dead to the world. Asleep—in this earth, at the least.

Theo squinted and focused on the open pages of the book. He jerked back down and sucked in the frigid winter air. It couldn't be. They were too late.

Annelee tugged at his shirt. "What's wrong? Is the book in there?"

"See for yourself."

She inched up, peered into the room, held on for a moment, and then dropped down.

"There are four fingerprints!"

"I know. Mine, yours, Danny's, and I'm guessing Asher's. He's crossed over!" Theo whispered.

"What does this mean?"

"It means we have to get back to other earth. If the Shataiki are involved, then it can't be good. They're up to something. We have to stop them!"

"Get back? How? He's got the book!"

"We have to get in there and get it."

"Okay." Annelee stood, placed her hands on the glass, and pushed. "It's stuck!"

Theo pushed with her, but the window wouldn't move. Locked on the inside. What else had he expected?

She suddenly stopped, staring into the room.

"What's wrong?" He followed her eyes and gasped.

Two red eyes flew across the room toward Asher, glaring at them. The face was attached to a faint but very real furry black body that landed on Asher's chest.

"Shax," Theo breathed. The Shataiki tilted its head and sneered. "He's guarding the book."

Theo backed away from the window, horrified. Everything about this was wrong. Then he had a thought, a dark memory from earlier that day: "Even if it means finding you in your world, I will blind you."

"What now?" Annelee croaked.

But Theo didn't have an answer, so he said the first thing that came to mind.

"We're dead."

Theo lay in bed, wide-eyed. He hadn't slept a wink the whole night. His body ached, and the sheets were damp from his sweat. The world around him had fallen apart.

Asher had crossed over and Shax was now in this earth. If Shadow Man truly was involved, something terrible was going to happen to them all.

"Theo, time for school!"

He jerked up at the sound of his dad's voice coming from the bottom of the stairs.

"Coming!"

He scrambled from bed, rushed across the room, and threw on some clean clothes. Hopefully, Annelee was thinking more clearly than he was, or maybe Danny would have an idea.

Theo gathered his backpack, sack lunch, and Pop-Tart, determined to come off as normal as possible, despite the sweat on his palms and the bags under his eyes. The last thing he needed was for his dad to get all worked up.

Theo clicked his seatbelt in place. "So, Dad, did you get all those papers graded?"

"Sure did. That'll teach me to assign five-paragraph essays to four different classes. Did you find what you were looking for?"

Did his dad know? "Uh, what?"

"I heard you downstairs kind of late last night. Thirsty?"

Theo couldn't stand lying to his dad anymore, so he smiled and changed the subject.

"Hey, Dad?" he asked as they pulled into the school parking lot. "Do you think I could have Annelee and Danny over for a sleepover tonight?"

"A sleepover? I don't think we've ever done one of those!"

"Yeah, we have to work on a big project, so I thought it might be fun to have them over for the night."

"Can a girl sleep over without it being weird? Not sure Annelee's parents will go for it."

He hadn't thought about that. Annelee might not even go for it.

"She can sleep on the bed! Danny and I'll take

the floor. We're just friends, so it won't be weird or anything." It actually was kind of weird. He'd never had a friend sleep over before, let alone a girl. But they needed time to think, together. Forty-five minutes at lunch under the supervision of the Grauberger wasn't enough time to figure out how to get back to other earth without the book.

"Well, I guess I can call Annelee's dad at lunch, and I'll pop over to Danny's foster mom's room on my break. Sound good?"

Theo was beginning to worry that neither of the families would allow it. "I think I need these kinds of things now. You know, time with my friends. With Mom being gone and all . . ." It was true.

"I get it. Okay, I'll make it happen." His dad smiled. "Sleepover it is."

"Thanks, Dad."

Theo jumped out of the car and headed full speed into the school. He pushed through the doors and darted toward his classroom. To his surprise Danny was sitting at his desk, waiting for him. Annelee entered right behind him.

"What are you two doing here so early?" Theo asked, sitting down across from Danny.

"My foster mom said I could come on to class."

Annelee took the seat in front of him. "I had my dad bring me today. Didn't feel like riding the bus."

Theo understood. He never felt like riding the bus and was thankful his dad could bring him every day.

"So?" Danny asked. "What happened last night?"

Theo took a deep breath, ready to speak, but Annelee spoke up first.

"Asher was there with the book. His blood was on the page. We couldn't get the book because a Shataiki is protecting him."

"Shax," Theo muttered under his breath.

"Seriously? So, what now?"

"I don't know yet, but I've asked my dad if you two can spend the night tonight so that we can figure this out."

Annelee crossed her arms. "A sleepover? My parents will never go for it."

"My dad's going to ask them. I told them I could use the time with friends, you know, since my mom and all. What we're facing here is way bigger than anyone could guess. We have to figure it out."

She nodded. "Well, there is that."

Danny spoke up. "I've never even been invited to a sleepover."

Theo frowned. "Me neither."

"Really?" Annelee said, cocking her brow and bringing the boys back to the moment. "I'm the queen of sleepovers. A little nail polish, some fashion magazines, a lot of talking, and the night takes care of itself!"

Both Theo and Danny chuckled nervously. That's not at all what Theo had in mind.

"What fun is happening in here?" Mrs. Baily asked, walking into the classroom. "It's kind of early for the two of you."

"Sorry, Mrs. Baily," Annelee said.

"No need to be sorry. It's nice to see that Theo isn't alone."

"Not anymore," Danny said.

First period came and went faster than Theo thought it would. Before he knew it, they were in the hallway, headed out to lunch to plan for the night.

"Hey, Asher! Where you been?"

The three spun at the voice of one of Asher's goons—Billy Carter.

Asher didn't respond. He just kept walking toward them from the end of the hall. The dark circles under his eyes had deepened, and his skin looked thin and pale.

Billy grabbed onto Asher's arm, trying to get his attention. Asher stopped. He paused for a few seconds and then abruptly turned around and shoved Billy against the locker.

"Don't touch me!"

Billy slunk down to the floor, clutching his bloody elbow.

Asher moved forward, walking down the hall in their direction. He shook his arm. Blood dripped to the floor. His elbow was bleeding exactly in the same spot Billy had been hurt.

"So he's not in other earth right now," Annelee whispered. "We can get the book before he goes back."

"Easier said than done," Theo said under his breath.

Asher stopped a few feet from them and stared with hollow eyes. It was as if he wasn't completely there, as if he was Asher but not Asher, as if someone or something else had taken up residence inside of him—something dark.

"You touch the book, and I'll kill you." Asher chuckled. "There are so many who want you dead, Theo Dunnery. And I thought I was the only one."

Theo swallowed hard and tried his best to appear strong, despite the fear rolling through him.

"Nobody's killing anyone," Annelee said, stepping in front of Theo.

"Oh, don't worry, ugly princess. They don't like you much either. Or you." Asher gestured toward

Danny and offered a weak grin. "This will be fun, friends."

With that, he walked past them, turned the corner, and vanished from sight.

"This isn't going to be good," Danny said.

For the rest of the day, Theo found himself repeatedly looking over his shoulder, sure that something was stalking him. He had three of the five seals, he knew about the light and Elyon, but he was still terrified. Why weren't they giving him the power he'd once felt?

That evening, Theo and Danny waited for Annelee to arrive while his dad ordered another pizza. Pizza two nights in a row was unheard of in the Dunnery house, unless it was leftovers.

"What's taking her so long?" Danny asked.

"I don't know, girl stuff I guess." Theo glanced at the clock on the DVD player: 6:32. Where was she?

At seven o'clock the doorbell rang. The boys raced for the door. Theo flung it open to find Annelee standing in polka-dot pajama pants and a heavy coat, carrying a pillow, a duffle bag, and a fuzzy blanket.

"What took you so long?" he asked, reaching for her belongings.

"I had to shower, pack, and take care of a couple house chores."

"Dad, Annelee's here!" he yelled. "We're gonna grab the pizza and head upstairs to work!"

"Okay! Let me know if you need anything!" his dad called from the back of the house.

The three trudged upstairs with Annelee holding the box, Danny feeling his way up the steps, and Theo behind them, carrying Annelee's bag. Theo dropped the bag on the bed and faced them.

"Asher's at home with the book right now. Probably crossing over again. We have to find a way. Any ideas?"

"The last two times, Stokes showed up and told you it was time to come, right?" Danny asked.

"Right."

"Okay, just thinking out loud here," Annelee said, grabbing a slice of pizza from the box. "You didn't have to put your blood on the page the last two times. So maybe you can travel whenever you want once your blood is in the book."

"Sure, but how? I've only ever gone using the book."

"So without the book, we're out of luck," Danny said. "Which means you have to get back over to Asher's and get the book, plain and simple."

Theo shook his head. "I told you, Shax is guarding it."

"Yeah, but if someone innocent, say a boy with

a cane who happens to be blind, were to show up at the front door asking to see Asher, even his parents wouldn't send me packing, right?"

They both looked at him.

"Then what?" Annelee asked.

"Then I show his parents what he's doing. And while they're still in shock, I grab the book, whack that Shataiki upside the head with my cane, and cross over before anyone can stop me."

"We can't let his parents—" Theo was cut short by a loud thump coming from the bathroom.

"Ouch!" a voice cried.

The bedroom door handle rattled and suddenly flew open. A white fluff ball with a small satchel hanging from his neck walked into the room.

"Stokes!" Annelee and Theo both shouted.

Stokes rubbed his bottom. "Rough landing."

Theo picked up Stokes, hugged him tightly, and then set him down.

"Asher has the book, Theo."

"I know! This wasn't supposed to happen. He'll bring Shadow Man and all the Shataiki to this world. Not good. Not good at all!"

Stokes didn't deny Theo's assumption.

Theo sat down on the edge of the bed. He had confirmed his worst fear. Shadow Man was coming for him.

"Unless Asher is stopped," Stokes continued, "all will be lost. But you can stop him. That's why I'm here, to ask you if you are willing to help."

"Yes, of course!" Annelee said.

"I'm in." Danny said.

"Theo?" Stokes asked.

Theo looked up. He couldn't let Shadow Man or the Shataiki into his world. There was no telling what they'd do to him or anyone else. "When can we go?"

"Right now."

"How?" Annelee asked.

"Oh, yes!" Stokes turned his satchel upside down. Four vials tumbled onto the bed—three clear, one purple. He picked up one of the clear vials.

"This is water from the green lakes. Drink this! You will sleep here and wake up in other earth."

Theo stared at the vials. "What's the purple one for?"

"Talya gave me that one to protect. It is a cure for the blinding dust."

"Blinding dust?" Danny asked.

"Shataiki use blinding dust in battle to weaken their opponents. Maybe it will have the opposite effect on Danny in this world."

Stokes popped the top off the vial and flung some of the purple dust at Danny's eyes.

Danny coughed and fanned the purple haze away from his face.

"Can you see?"

"Nope, still blind. But thanks, it was worth a try."

"Hmmm . . . oh well." Stokes put the vial back in his satchel. "Ready?"

Theo picked up one of the clear vials and handed it to Danny, who

immediately pulled off the top and sniffed. Theo picked up another one, and Annelee, the last.

"Oh, and once you get there, you must find Shadow Man's lair. That's where Asher will most likely be. Find the highest point in other earth, and his lair is beneath that."

"You're not coming with us?" Theo asked.

"I have other very important business. But you know your way around now, yes? As Talya says, follow your heart. Drink the water and find yourself in other earth."

Theo held up the vial. "Just like that?"

"How else?"

"Well then, here goes nothing." Theo took a sip from the vial. The sweet warm water trickled into his mouth and filled him with the familiar feeling of power and peace.

"See you on the other side," Stokes said, biting into the fruit that helped him to travel between earths.

The room began to fade in and out. Theo yawned. His eyes grew heavy. He felt his body fall onto his bed. And then he slept.

The soft sound of rustling leaves filled Theo's ears as the sweet aroma invaded his nostrils. He opened his eyes wide. The mountain he had climbed on his last three quests stood in front of him. He was back.

Tree branches swayed in the wind above him. If only he could stay here all day doing nothing but watching those branches; however, he didn't have that luxury today.

He sat up to find Annelee and Danny waking up as well.

Danny stretched, opened his eyes, and grinned. He jumped up and threw his arms wide. "I can see again!"

Annelee, who hadn't been there the first time Danny gained his sight, jumped up and joined him, giggling and dancing like a girl much younger than she was. "You can see? You can really see? Just like that?"

Danny stopped and faced her. "Theo's right, you really are beautiful. But I knew that before I saw you with my eyes."

She blushed, stammering for her next words. She glanced at Theo, who had his head buried in his hands. "I . . . um . . . Isn't it *all* so beautiful?" she cried, sweeping her arms and spinning around.

"Amazing," Danny said, turning in circles to take it all in again.

"Not to break this up," Theo said, clearing his throat and recovering from his embarrassment, "but we've got to figure out what to do next."

"You're right. For a moment, I almost forgot why we came back."

Annelee plopped down next to Theo. "Stokes said to find Shadow Man's lair. The word alone makes it sound like a pretty terrible place."

Theo remembered the first level of his last quest and cringed. He'd had enough of Shadow Man's hangouts. "But I'm not sure we should go just yet. I think we should find Talya. We only have the first three seals. Without the last two, I'm not sure we can stop Shadow Man for good. I've always gone to Talya first. He gives me the quest and leads me to the door."

"But is this a quest?" she asked. "Don't we have to

deal with Shadow Man now?"

"I'm supposed to find all five seals," he said, standing. "This has to be part of my quest for the last two."

"Or maybe stopping Asher is the way to the seals," Danny said.

Silence filled the grassy clearing as Theo paced back and forth. "We should go to Talya. I really think it's important."

Annelee accepted Danny's offered hand and stood. "I trust Theo."

"I do too."

Theo liked their confidence in him. But he wasn't as certain with his decision as they were.

"It's settled then," he said. "We find the rest of the seals, and then we find Asher." He pulled up his sleeve to be reminded by the glowing symbol on his shoulder. "White: Elyon is the light without darkness. He is all powerful and cannot be threatened."

"Green," Annelee said, stepping up to him. "We are the light of the world but often don't know because we are blind to who we are."

"Black," Danny said, joining them. "Our journey is to see the light in the darkness. When we don't, it's because we're seeing through the wrong lenses."

"We have to remember," Theo said. "We can't forget them." He was talking more to himself than to the others. "Alright then, onward to the mountain door!"

An hour later they stood in silence before the giant double doors carved into the rock. Nervous energy tickled Theo's arms and spine even though he'd already passed through these doors three times. He would have thought he'd be used to this all by now, but he wasn't.

They walked down the hall of torches and into the room of the five colored doors. He'd gone through the first three and found a seal each time. But that was before Asher had stolen the book.

"Good to see you," a low voice said from their right. Talya was leaning against a rock, arms crossed, smiling. His kind eyes swept Theo with a gentle peace. "I'm so glad all of you have chosen to come back despite the predicament you find yourselves in."

Theo lowered his eyes. "Talya, I'm so sorry. This is all my fault. If I had just—"

"This isn't your fault," Annelee snapped. "It's Asher's!"

"We'll stop him," Danny said.

They were both so strong, so sure. He might be wiser because of the seals he'd found, but Theo felt weak standing next to them.

"This is no one's fault," Talya said, approaching them. "You will understand this truth when you find the last two seals."

"Two?" Theo asked. He'd been right. This was a quest.

"Yes, for these last two seals, you'll need to learn that there is no fear in love. It's a terribly hard lesson for most to comprehend much less experience. Regardless, know that you won't be able to stop Asher without all five seals, so you'd best hurry. Remember, you are the light of the world, but so is Asher."

Theo wanted to contradict Talya, to tell him the truth. Asher was a bully. He'd called Annelee an ugly princess on more than one occasion and probably would have punched her in the face had Mr. O'Brian not been there to stop him. And he took *The Book of History*. There wasn't an ounce of light inside of Asher. The thought of him made Theo's heart race and his stomach tighten. He hated Asher Brox.

Talya placed a hand on Theo's shoulder. "Theo, my friend, you must surrender this darkness. When you judge another, you judge yourself and join the very darkness that you condemn."

Theo knew better than to push any question with Talya. He said only what was meant to be said and no more.

"It's time to go, my brave friends."

Talya studied them each with a look that made Theo wonder just how brave they would have to be. Was it pity in Talya's eyes or pride? Theo couldn't tell.

"Your quest awaits." Talya pointed his staff toward the red door. The torches lit on each side, illuminating above it a red cross, equal on all four sides.

"Whatever's behind this door, we handle it together," Annelee said, grabbing Theo's and Danny's hands.

But Theo pulled back and turned to Talya. "What if we fail?"

"You must not."

Theo took a swift breath and pushed the door open. The familiar light gushed toward him from within. It quickly pulled them in, swirling them in the light they knew so well.

They reached the end of the tunnel quicker than Theo would have liked, dumping them on hard ground. The door vanished, leaving them alone.

Theo sprang to his feet and spun around, taking in his surroundings. It was another large, hot, sandy desert with nothing in sight but a giant mountain far in the distance. The ominous black mountain reached high into the sky, piercing the clouds above it.

Theo's gut churned at the sight. Asher was close. So was Shadow Man.

"That's it," Danny said, eyes round with fear. The joy of seeing had turned on him.

"Shadow Man's lair," Annelee said. "They weren't joking about the tallest mountain. The peak is literally in the clouds."

The three stared, silent.

It was Danny who interrupted their awe. "Well?"

Theo took charge, trying to be strong. "Let's go."

"Just go?" Annelee huffed. "Talya didn't give us much direction this time. I mean, how do we find both the seals? Finding one of them was hard enough, and now we have to find two before we can stop Asher?"

"Should we even go to the mountain then?" Danny asked. "If we can't stop Asher without the seals, then why go?"

"I don't know," Theo said. "You have a better idea? This is where the door brought us—where Talya sent us. It just so happens to also be where Stokes told us to find the mountain. We found it, so we go."

In all honesty, Theo had no idea how they would find the seals or stop Asher. But he did know that avoiding danger wasn't in their future. They had to go and then see what happened.

"Wait." Danny pointed at the sky. "You guys see that?"

Theo followed Danny's finger and saw that something was flying toward them in the distance. From where they stood, it looked like a big black smudge of a beast, gliding across the sky. But as it came closer and into focus, Theo's body quickly tensed.

"That can't be real," Annelee said in disbelief.

Shataiki!

But it wasn't just any Shataiki. It was a giant Theo had met once before: Ruza—the beast with the scarred eye and torn nose.

On its back sat a rider glaring at them as it neared, eyes locked on Theo. Theo knew that rider.

It was Asher.

The beast landed in front of them. Asher slid off, landing with a thud that sent dust flying into the air. A wicked smile twisted his face. Whatever weakness had ravaged his body in the other world was gone here. Dark circles still hung under his eyes, and his elbow was crusted with blood from the incident in the hallway earlier that day. But in every other way, Asher looked as if he'd gained muscles and height overnight.

He stopped a few paces from them and, with feet planted in the sand, slowly started clapping. The clap boomed around them, sending shivers up Theo's neck.

"Congratulations! You made it here without the book. Shadow Man said you'd figure it out, but I was betting against you maggots."

Annelee crossed her arms and narrowed her eyes. "Asher, give us the book and go home!"

The wicked smile twitched on Asher's face as a gravelly chuckle shook his body.

"I'd rather not. You see, I've never felt better in my life. There's a new energy, a power, that's rushing through my body, and I gotta say . . . I love it."

Asher suddenly shot up into the air, soared high above them, and then came crashing down to earth. He landed inches from Annelee before she quickly retreated backward.

Theo's stomach turned. He knew the three of them were reeking with fear, and Asher was breathing it in with delight.

Asher burst into hard chuckles as he straightened his body and began to walk in circles around them, like a hyena waiting to devour its prey.

Theo remembered. "I am the light! I am the son of Elyon! Nothing can—"

Asher's hard cackling halted Theo. Theo tried to speak to finish saying what he knew, but it wouldn't come out. The cackling echoed in his mind. All he could think about was the memory and pain of Asher's fist connecting with his face.

"Shadow Man asked me to set up a little game for him, and I couldn't resist. You guys wanna play?"

Theo's blood boiled. All he wanted to do was punch Asher square in the jaw, but he knew he would lose that battle the minute Asher recovered from the blow. He had always been weaker than Asher, and seeing him now, he knew there was no hope.

"We're not playing your game," Theo said.

"Did you hear that?" Asher asked the Shataiki. "Theo doesn't want to play." He turned to Theo. "Oh, come on. Have a little fun with me."

Theo ignored Asher and started to walk away.

"No?" Asher sneered. "Well then, how about you, Danny? Do you want to play?"

Theo spun back around to see Asher swiftly reach into his pocket and pull out a handful of black powder. Asher grinned and thrust his hand forward, releasing the powder into Danny's face. A black cloud began to twirl around Danny's head. Then it drilled itself straight into his eyes and vanished.

Danny screamed and fell to the ground, rubbing his eyes frantically. "It burns! It burns!"

The huge Shataiki snickered.

Theo took three long steps and planted himself between Danny and Asher. He stared directly at his enemy. Annelee tried to help Danny as he screamed in pain, but Theo knew there was nothing she could do for him. Asher wanted him to suffer. And he was getting what he wanted.

"This game is going to be so much fun," Asher said as he cocked his head, looking at Theo without any sense of fear or regret.

"What did you do him?" Theo demanded.

"It was just a little dust. He'll be fine." A smile spread wide across his face. "That is, if he finds the cure in time."

"Cure?" Danny asked.

Annelee jumped to her feet. "And what if he doesn't?"

"Well, he goes blind again here, but the fun part is that apparently something quite different happens back home." Asher savored the moment and then smiled in Danny's direction. "If you don't find the cure in twenty-four hours, he won't have eyes at all back home. They'll burn out and take some of your brain, too. And who knows what that will do to you."

"You're a monster," Theo growled.

"Don't worry, Danny," Annelee said, helping him to his feet. "We know who has a cure."

"Oh, do you mean your little fluff-ball friend?" Asher laughed. "Yeah, I took care of him too." He shoved his chin to the mountain range opposite them. "You'll find him over there. Wonder how long those ropes hold before they burn up." He shrugged. "Oh well."

Danny stumbled toward Asher with blood-shot eyes. "I can still see, and I will find Stokes. You haven't won!"

"You'll be blind before you get there," Asher said and turned to walk away. "Oh, and one last thing." He spun back. "You have twenty-four hours to save her before I make her like me."

Her?

Before Theo could register who "her" was, Asher rushed up to Annelee, grabbed her by one wrist and jerking her toward the Shataiki he'd flown in on.

"Stop it!" she cried, kicking and punching. "Theo!"

"Annelee!" Danny screamed, racing past Theo, who stood frozen as he watched her being thrown onto Ruza's back. Before Danny was even half way to Ruza, Asher and Annelee were on the bat's back.

"The choice is yours," Asher called down to them. "Who will you save? Danny or Annelee?"

Ruza sprang from the ground, taking Asher and Annelee with him. Theo watched them slowly fade into the distance until he saw nothing but blue sky. He fell to his knees, swallowed up with terrible guilt and confusion. How could he have let this happen? He didn't even try to stop Asher!

Danny walked over to Theo, jaw firm. "My sight's

fading. We have to get the cure before it's gone."

"And what, let them have Annelee?"

"I'm not saying that, but I'm more helpful to you with sight than without. Matter of fact, I'm useless if I'm dead. Asher made it pretty clear what would happen to me in the other world if we don't get the cure. I like my brain! Besides, we have to save Stokes! He can help us save Annelee."

Theo knew he was right. He didn't want anything bad to happen to Danny or Stokes, but what was going to happen to Annelee? He couldn't imagine her becoming like Asher.

"We need to get going. There has to be a way to save us both, but it's not sitting here doing nothing."

Theo grabbed Danny's outstretched hand. "You're right," he said, standing to his feet. "We have to do something or both of you . . ." He stopped, unwilling to speak what he and Danny already knew.

Asher had set Shadow Man's evil game in motion, and Theo was the main player. The choice was his: save Danny or save Annelee. If one of them died, it would be his fault.

Neither Theo nor Danny spoke as they walked. Theo did his best not to think about Annelee and what Asher was doing to her, but the thoughts gnawed at his brain without end. They had less than twenty-four hours to save her, and they were headed in the wrong direction.

Danny had been right; they needed Stokes. So that was the plan. Save Stokes. Heal Danny. Find Annelee.

They plodded across the desert in silence, headed toward the mountain range Asher had shown them, growing wider and larger as the hours passed. Theo wiped sweat from his forehead. It was so hot. His body ached.

Whispers of fear invaded his mind. What if he had made the wrong choice? What if they didn't make it to Stokes in time? What if Annelee . . .

"Theo," Danny's voice rasped behind him. "I can barely see. I don't think we're going to make it."

Theo had been so worried about Annelee that he hadn't thought much about how scary this was for Danny. At this very moment his brain was being consumed by the blinding dust both here and at home.

"You're going to be all right," he said with as much confidence as he could. "We're almost there."

"Unless Asher sent us on a wild goose chase. Maybe I'm supposed to die this way, believing I can be saved. What if it's all a joke? What if it's all part of Shadow Man's plan? Trick the blind boy!"

"No! Don't talk that way!" Theo touched his arm. He could not forget. "Listen to me, Danny. Even when we're afraid, we have to remember who we are! We're the light of the world. We have the Kingdom glasses inside of us, remember? We can see through them if we remind ourselves who we truly are. Remember the seals!"

"I'm going blind!" Danny cried. "I can't see anything, much less the Kingdom. What if it takes less than twenty-four hours for the dust to work? Asher's not the sharpest tool in the shed. Times running out for me! I can feel it!"

Theo hesitated. He didn't really know what else

to say. Although he knew the truths of the seals, he was having a hard time believing them himself.

"Well, we have to at least try. Come on. I'll guide you."

They trekked through the desert for another hour, closing the distance to the rising mountains. Every step took them farther from Shadow Man's lair where Asher was doing only Elyon knew what to Annelee.

A glimpse of truth passed through Theo. Hope. Then it was gone.

It was with some surprise that Theo noticed they were no longer walking through sand but on flat rock. That rock quickly led them into a massive canyon at the base of the mountain range.

Hope began to swell in Theo again. They were getting close. They had to be!

And then he could feel the heat rising from the rock floor of the canyon. It was like they were nearing some kind of volcano or something.

"Do you feel that?"

"It's getting hotter," Danny said. "I felt it a ways back."

"Asher said something about burning ropes. We have to be close. Can you see anything?"

"Nope!"

"Sorry. I forgot."

Danny didn't say anything else. How frustrating it must be to see one minute and then be blind the next. Another glimpse of truth passed through him.

"Hold onto my arm." Theo quickened his pace with Danny in tow. It was now up to him to get the cure and save them all. The what-ifs tore at his thoughts. The pressure was almost more than he could take.

As they came around a bend in the canyon, Theo saw a large opening in one of the rock walls. Without another thought, he headed straight for that opening and led Danny into the tunnel, ignoring the fear that whispered in his head.

Danny stopped short, jerking Theo back. "Do you hear that?"

Theo tried to listen, but he didn't hear anything.

"It's like a whistle or something. Up ahead. Close your eyes and try again."

Theo did as Danny asked. Then he heard it—a smooth, high-pitched whistle. And then, "Help! Please! Anyone!"

"Stokes! It's him!" Danny said.

Theo began to jog, practically dragging Danny behind him. Soon the tunnel led out to a large room tucked deep into the mountain. There hung Stokes, dangling from a rope tied to a giant spike jutting from the ceiling.

Theo pulled to a stop. Danny bumped into him from behind.

"What?" Danny whispered. "You see him?"

Theo coughed and covered his nose. "He's hanging over a pit of lava."

Danny took a step back. "It smells like rotten eggs! What else do you see?"

"So, we're kind of on a ledge, but there's an old wooden bridge suspended from here to the other side. And there's a platform in the middle connected to the bridge. He's directly above it."

Stokes looked up, eyes round and swimming in relief. "Theo! Danny! Oh, thank Elyon! Thank Elyon! You must save me! Asher was waiting for me when I returned and ambushed me before I could defend myself. It was too quick! I'm so sorry, I—"

"It's okay, Stokes," Theo called over the rumbling boil of the lava. "Don't struggle or you might loosen the ropes and fall. We'll get you down."

"What should I do?" Danny asked.

"Stay here and don't move. You're safe where you are. One slip and you might be swimming in burning lava, and then we won't need the cure anymore."

"What are you going to do?" Danny asked, feeling for the wall and then holding it tightly.

Theo took a deep breath, trying to push away the

fear. "I'm going to cross the bridge and try to reach Stokes."

"Be careful!" Stokes trembled, his fur ruffled and matted. What else had Asher done to him? "The bridge is very old."

"I can see that." His heart pounded as he grabbed the two posts connecting the bridge to the ledge. Holding his breath, he slowly placed his right foot onto the first plank of wood. It seemed strong enough, so he inched his left foot forward.

He stood motionless with his full weight on the bridge. Nothing happened. One foot after the other, he stepped forward, praying each piece of wood would hold him. The bridge creaked and popped but held.

"It sounds like it might break," Danny rasped. "Maybe you should just run across. Get it over with."

Stokes immediately objected. "No, just one step at a time in case the wood—"

A loud snap echoed around the cavern. Theo felt the wood give way beneath his feet. Then his body dropped. He threw his arm around the next board and caught himself, dangling over the lava. He could hear Stokes screaming something, but Theo was too focused on not dying to make out what he was saying.

He pulled his body up with his left hand, securing his right on the plank. He inhaled, gagging on the sulfuric fumes, and tried to pull his body up on the bridge. Another snap. He exhaled, fingers gripping the splintering wood.

"Hold on! I'm coming!" Danny cried.

"No!" Theo shouted, trying to pull himself up again. "It's too dangerous." Sweat poured down his cheeks, possibly mixed with a tear or two, and his lungs burned. If he died here, he'd die back home. Theo pulled again, but his arms weren't strong enough.

The bridge creaked and swayed. Danny was coming for him. Theo didn't know whether to think of him as brave this time or stupid.

He could feel his hands slipping. He was too petrified to think straight much less tell Danny to slow down. The lava was bubbling hot below him, heating up his Converse, warming his feet, and most likely melting the soles.

"Hurry, Danny!" Stokes yelled.

Then a hand was on Theo's arm, yanking him up. With Danny's help, Theo hauled himself up on the bridge and sprawled out on the old wooden planks, breathing heavily.

"Thank you." He coughed, gasping for breath in the heated air. "But how did you—"

"I crawled . . . carefully."

Theo didn't want to move. He wanted to sit in the safety of the moment for as long as possible.

A *snap*! And another *crack*!

They had no choice. "We have to get off this bridge." Theo coughed again, pulling his T-shirt up over his nose. "We'll stay on all fours, like you did, and move quickly. It seems safer that way."

Scrambling on all fours, they both made it to the platform below Stokes without another board breaking.

Freeing Stokes was a simple matter. While Danny held his body, Theo untied the rope. The moment Stokes was free, he stretched out his wings and leaped into the air. He soared around, did a flip as if checking to see that he was whole, and then landed heavily next to the boys.

"Thanks for saving me!" he cried, hugging each with his wings. "I've been whistling for help for hours but nothing gets past all this rock."

Danny was eager. "Do you have that purple dust Talya gave you?"

"You're blind?" Stokes reached into his satchel and pulled it out. "Of course! Of course!"

Theo took the vile from Stokes's hand, popped the cork, and poured some of the dust into his hand.

"How does it work?"

"Blow it into his eyes."

Theo did as Stokes instructed. The purple dust hovered in front of Danny's face and then evaporated into his eyes.

"Anything?"

Danny blinked, and then he pumped a fist into the air. "I can see!" He glanced down and then quickly inched closer to Theo. "So that's lava. I think I was better not seeing it."

Theo let out a long breath of relief. He'd saved

two of his friends. Now he only hoped he had time to save Annelee.

"Who blinded you?" Stokes asked. "What happened?"

"A lot. But first, let's get out of this place." Theo turned to head back.

Neither needed further encouragement. Danny and Theo crawled back across the wooden bridge while Stokes took to the air. Once across, they hurried from the pit of lava.

They took off through the tunnel toward the entrance, but that was as far as they got. Something had changed. A door that Theo was certain hadn't been there before was set into the canyon wall across from them. But it was a door he had seen before—the fifth door—the white door with a tiny pearl-like circle above it.

"How can that be?" Danny asked.

"I have no idea," Theo said.

"We don't have the fourth seal yet." Danny turned round eyes to Theo. "Do we?"

Theo pulled up his sleeve—no fourth seal, only the first three: white, green, and black. "No. That's odd."

Danny headed for the door. "Maybe we should go through it. Talya wouldn't send it here if we weren't supposed to."

Chapter 5

He had a good point. Maybe this door would lead them closer to Annelee.

"Try it," Stokes said. "It must be what Talya wants."

Theo placed his hands on the white wooden door and pushed it open. Light burst from inside. It pulled them through, wrapping them in its warmth as they fell freely into the light.

Theo clambered to his feet and looked up at the black rocky mass in front of them. The door had dumped them on cold, hard sand, shadowed by the mountain that reached into the clouds. A twinge of panic rushed through him as an icy breeze brushed against his skin.

Danny stood and stared up with round eyes. "Is that—?"

"The highest peak," Theo finished.

"Shadow Man's lair," Stokes rasped. "The door has brought us to a very wicked place."

"Annelee." The thought of her in that awful place spun through Theo's mind. "We need to find our way in and save her before it's too late."

Danny faced him. "But how do we get in without being seen? What if this is a trap?"

Theo felt rattled and scared. Anger and revenge boiled in his gut.

Asher.

"Doesn't matter. We have to save her. We've wasted way too much time already."

Danny looked away.

"I . . . I didn't mean for it to come out that way." Theo knew the diversion to save Stokes and Danny wasn't their fault, but he couldn't help but blame them a little. Danny should have closed his eyes the minute he saw Asher pull out the powder. And Stokes was a warrior; he should never have been captured in the first place.

"We should have been more careful," Stokes said apologetically.

"No, it's not your fault," Theo assured him, still slightly annoyed.

"If it's any help, I think I know a way in that will keep us hidden," Stokes said, breaking the tense moment. "There should be a side tunnel that leads down into the lair."

"How do you know?" Danny asked.

"Michal and Gabil have examined this lair with great care," Stokes said proudly. "Remember when Talya gave them a special mission last time you were here? It was to understand the ins and outs of this horrible place. That's when they found it! A secret way in."

New energy rushed through Theo. "So Talya knew we would be here."

"Clearly. But it will be dangerous. If not, Talya wouldn't have gone to such lengths to prepare us."

"So take us there!" Danny insisted.

"Follow me." Stokes took to the air and flew forward to the right side of the mountain.

Theo glanced over at Danny. "I shouldn't have said . . . I didn't mean that . . ." It was his best attempt at an apology. Asher was trying to divide them. It was all part of Shadow Man's game.

Theo had fallen into their trap. He wouldn't let it happen again.

Danny offered him a thin smile before taking off after their fluffy leader.

Stokes led them around the right side of the mountain and then landed inches from the rocky wall. Before them was a large crack in the black stone. At the bottom of the crack was a hole large enough for a boy to squeeze into. Or a Roush.

Stokes stepped back and crossed his wings, impressed with himself. "This will lead to Shadow Man's lair."

"Perfect," Danny said.

"Or not so perfect," Theo said. "It looks pretty dark in there."

"Then I'll lead. I'm used to darkness, remember?"

Without another beat they were squeezing into the opening, one after the other, led by Danny. After about ten feet, the narrow gap opened to a large tunnel.

As Theo had assumed, it was dark and the temperature had dropped. A foul scent of Shataiki filled the dank air. His skin prickled with goose bumps as he tried to shake off the feeling of dread that came with them.

"Actually, maybe I should lead from here," Stokes whispered. "I can see in darkness much more than you humans."

"Okay," Danny willingly agreed.

Theo didn't blame Danny for giving up the lead. There was a feeling that hung in the air—dark and foul.

They followed close to Stokes as he weaved his way through the darkness. But it wasn't long before Theo saw a slight glow at the end of the tunnel. All three stopped and stared ahead. A low chuckle drifted from deep inside the mountain.

Shadow Man.

"Careful," Stokes whispered, heading toward the dimly lit cavern. He crouched as he approached the opening. Together, they edged past.

Theo's pulse raced as he took in the sight in front

of him. It was a large cavern lined with thousands of Shataiki, most hanging from the walls like bats. They were all focused on the scene in the middle of the lair. But the object of their fixation was hidden by a ledge.

"Easy," Stokes said, edging forward to the lip of the ledge.

They followed him on all fours and then peeked over the edge into the bowels of the lair.

Asher stood at the center of the cavern below as Shadow Man lurked around him, watching.

Then Theo saw Annelee. She was lying unmoving on a bed-like platform a few feet away from Asher and Shadow Man.

Danny gasped. "That's her!"

Theo could feel the blood drain from his face. He prayed she was asleep and not dead.

Shadow Man's voice filled the cavern. "Tell us again, Asher, what are you going to do?"

Theo's chest tightened at the sound of the voice.

"I will make her like me, and she will be mine," Asher answered. "I will finish what you have started."

The Shataiki screeched and howled in response.

"Yes," Shadow Man hissed, walking over to Annelee's motionless body. "Our sleeping beauty will be very helpful when the time comes. It takes two in agreement to create the bridge. You will take her back to your world and create a way for me and my legions to infect that world with a fear so dark they will never see light again."

The Shataiki all around him shrilled again in delight. Theo felt Danny's hand grab onto his shoulder.

He watched as Shadow Man brushed his filthy fingers across Annelee's cheek. If not for Danny's hand on his shoulder, he might have bolted to his feet and run to stop him, however insane that would've been.

"There are only two true powers in the world, Asher: fear and love. We despise love, but fear we live for." Shadow Man paused, placing his hands on Asher's shoulders. "Do you know why I want to come over to your world?"

"No, why?" Asher asked.

"Because most people in your world are blind to the depths of their fear. I plan on showing them who they really are. I will make that world like mine, and I will rule them both."

Shadow Man's wicked grin twitched his face as he motioned toward the bed. Asher returned his smirk, obeying.

"Sleep now, Asher, and do what must be done."

Asher walked over to the bed where Annelee slept. He lay down next to her and closed his eyes. Theo felt sick to his stomach.

He jumped at the tug to his sleeve and turned to see Danny and Stokes sneaking back the way they'd come. He looked back at Annelee one more time and then quickly followed them down the tunnel, through the crack, and back into the night air outside the mountain.

Theo ground his teeth and then let out a scream. He kicked up some sand and threw his fist against the cool breeze.

"We can't save her!" he said, swallowed up by rage. But this time, the rage was for himself more than Asher. He felt completely useless. There was no way to defeat such a powerful army of beasts.

Stokes waddled over to Theo and grabbed his hand with a tiny pink finger.

"We might not be able to do much here right now, but maybe you can still save Annelee in your world."

The Roush's words crashed into Theo's mind. Maybe they *could* save her back at home. Maybe they could stop whatever Shadow Man had planned for her before it ever happened.

"It might work," Danny said. "We could save Annelee back home!"

"Maybe," Theo said as he spun away from the black mountain. "We need to find a safe place to sleep so that we can wake up there. It might be the only way."

He didn't want to say what was really on his heart.

It might be too late.

Theo and Danny significantly distanced themselves from the towering mountain before they set up camp behind an outcropping of rock. Night was creeping toward them as the sun sank into the horizon. The plan was simple: fall asleep here and wake up back home to save Annelee.

If they could.

Stokes had left them to find a special kind of fruit, the Ruthja, which would help Theo and Danny fall asleep fast. With all the nervous energy flowing through them, falling asleep without it would be impossible.

"Maybe we should build a fire," Danny suggested. "I've got to do something! Just sitting here waiting for Stokes, I think I might go mad."

"Tell me about it," Theo said, picking up a stick that lay at his feet. With the sun fading, the desert was slowly losing its heat. "A fire sounds like a good idea."

All they needed was some dried grass, wood, and some sticks. Theo helped Danny gather sticks and brush and place them in a pile in the center of the clearing. He'd made a fire once with his dad on a weekend camping trip. It didn't seem so hard then. They'd used matches, but his dad had shown him how a fire could be made using flint.

He wondered what his dad was doing now. Had time passed a little or a lot this time? Had his dad found them all asleep? Had Annelee already woken up there?

He was so lost in his thoughts that the most obvious problem with making a fire only presented itself to him when he was about to give it all a whirl.

"Wait a minute! What if the fire attracts Shataiki?"

Danny dropped the firewood. "Oh, yeah. That wouldn't be good."

"Nope."

"So much for the fire."

"Yeah. So much for the fire."

Theo sat with Danny beside the pile of useless firewood, waiting. He tried to quiet his buzzing mind, but it was an impossible task. He shivered. The night was getting colder.

"What are we even going to do when we get back?" Danny asked, ending their stretch of silence.

"Hopefully Annelee is still asleep in my room. We have to wake her up and snap her out of whatever trance Shadow Man has her in."

"Unless Asher's already taken her. Let's cross our fingers she's still there. There's no telling how much time has passed."

Theo heard the sound of flapping wings. He spun to find Stokes flying toward them.

"You can't build a fire here," the Roush said, eyeing the firewood as he landed.

"We know."

"Sorry. It took me awhile to find these." Stokes pulled out two tiny blue fruits from his satchel. They looked exactly like blueberries. But Theo was sure, as with everything else in other earth, that they'd taste nothing like they looked.

He took one of the fruits. Stokes handed the other to Danny.

"You sleep," Stokes said. "I'll keep lookout."

"Just eat the fruit?" Danny asked.

"I'd lie down first," Stokes answered. "You don't want to fall over and hit your head."

"That fast?"

"That fast."

Theo and Danny found spots to sleep on the sand near the useless firewood and popped the tiny fruits into their mouths.

Sour, Theo thought. *Nothing like blueberry.* Then he closed his eyes.

When he opened them, he was back in his home world.

His room came into focus with The Vanisher poster hanging on the wall across from him. He shot up when his body finally connected to his mind. Danny was already on his feet, hand on the bed, feeling for Annelee.

Blind again.

"She isn't here, is she?" he asked.

The bed was empty. She was already gone?

"She can't be gone!" Theo ran to his door and jerked it open. The house was quiet. "Check the bathroom, and wait here!"

He raced down the stairs, hoping Annelee was in the house somewhere. He slid into the kitchen, but she wasn't there either. There was only one other place she could be—the living room.

Theo found Annelee there, sitting on the couch and staring at the blank TV screen. She looked pale and weak, like the victim of a vampire. She was here and that meant they could save her.

"Annelee?" Theo said, hurrying to her side. "Annelee, are you okay?"

Annelee sat motionless. She didn't even blink.

"What's wrong with her?" Danny asked, having ignored Theo's suggestion to wait.

"She doesn't look right. She looks kinda like Asher looked when we saw him at school yesterday—half dead."

Annelee slowly turned her head toward the two boys. She stared at them for what felt like a long minute and then spoke. "I have to leave now. I called

my mom to come pick me up. I'm not sure why I'm even here." She eyed him cautiously. "Theo. That's your name, right? What a loser."

Theo felt like a bag of bricks had landed on his chest. She didn't remember him? Did she even remember who *she* was?

He sat down beside her. "Annelee, you can't go. We have to get back before it's too late."

"I'd never be caught dead going anywhere with you two freaks," she said, standing. "Besides, I have something I have to do."

"Annelee, remember the seals?" Theo pleaded. "You know who you are."

He jumped to his feet and jerked her sleeve up to show her the seals. "You have to—"

Her tattoo was gone. She had lost the seals. She smirked at him and walked toward the door.

"Annelee," Danny said, grabbing onto her arm as she walked past him.

She spun toward Danny and effortlessly shoved him to the floor like a doll.

"Don't touch me, maggot!" She flipped her hair over her shoulder and resumed her exit.

Maggot? It sounded like something Asher would say.

What had Asher done to her?

"Well, good morning, boys and lady," Theo's dad

said, walking into the room. "I hate that you woke up feeling sick, Annelee. I'm sure your mom will be here any second."

The sound of two honks came from outside.

If she left, there was no hope of saving her in this world.

"Well, will you look at that?" his dad said. "Right on time."

"Please, Annelee, just stay a little longer," Theo begged.

"See you at school, Theo." Annelee smiled at him, opened the door, and was gone.

Theo felt sick.

"You boys want some breakfast?" his dad asked cheerfully.

Theo couldn't answer. He couldn't believe what had just happened.

"Maybe in a little bit, Mr. Dunnery," Danny said. "Theo and I have a game to finish playing upstairs. Right, Theo?"

Theo stood in shock.

"Theo?"

Theo's mind was elsewhere. "Actually, Danny, why don't you eat some breakfast with my dad. I'm going to grab some air outside, and then I'll join you."

"Son, are you okay?" his dad asked. "I hope you're not coming down with what Annelee has."

"No, I just need some fresh air."

Theo quickly opened the back door and exited the house. Shadow's Man game was spiraling out of control. He needed to breathe. He needed to think, and he knew just where to go.

He made his way straight to the tree house his dad had built for him shortly after his mom died. It was supposed to be Theo's alone space, his place to think and cry if needed—his place of comfort away from the house. He'd spent hours writing notes to his mom, drawing pictures of the two of them and then sticking them all over the walls. But he hadn't been up in the tree house in months.

He grabbed onto the makeshift ladder and climbed into the tiny wooden shack nestled in the branches ten feet off the ground. He crawled in, sat on the floor, and allowed the horror of his situation to wash over him. She'd called him a loser.

He had to remember that it wasn't Annelee—not the Annelee he knew anyway. They'd done something to her.

He buried his head into his knees and tried to quiet the voices of accusation in his mind. Tears began to prick at his eyes, and his chest felt like it was filled with lead.

"Elyon," Theo whispered, "I'm so sorry. I failed you."

"You haven't failed me, Theo," a small voice said next to him.

Theo looked up from his knees to find himself no longer in his tree house but sitting on top of a hill overlooking his whole town. Beside him was the old swing set. On one of the swings sat the boy with beautiful, kind blue eyes that he'd met in other earth.

Theo scrambled to his feet. "Elyon?"

The boy smiled at Theo. A warm peace flooded Theo's body. Everything suddenly felt okay, as if there never had been nor ever would be a problem.

"You can never fail or disappoint me," the boy said, looking past Theo at the city.

Theo thought he should say something, but no words came.

"What do you see down there?" the boy asked, motioning toward the town.

Theo stared at the town he'd grown up in. It was a pretty big town, but he could see most of it from where he sat—his school, the little movie theater, his and his dad's favorite ice cream shop, and his house.

"It's my town," he said, his voice small. "And you're here, in my town!"

The boy laughed. "I'm everywhere. Did you forget?"

Theo had forgotten. But with this simple reminder, he envisioned the lion of sand, larger than the universe, surrounding him, so close he could almost breathe it.

The boy waved his hand over the town. "Take a closer look. Really look at it."

Theo squinted and focused on the buildings and the streets moving with cars and people like a giant gazing down at a city of ants. But as he observed, he noticed that something dark was moving. A thick black fog was flowing through the streets and into the doors and windows of every home.

"What is that?" Theo asked.

"Fear. Let's get a little bit closer."

The boy snapped his finger, and suddenly Theo was standing in one of his school hallways. The black fog surrounded him, and for a split second, Theo felt completely overwhelmed by fear. But then the boy took his hand and the fog parted where they stood.

"Most people live in fear like this all the time, but they're blind to it. It's so normal that they don't even realize that they can know a life without fear."

Theo watched as the fog seeped into lockers and under doors, consuming every nook and cranny in the school. He wondered how his classmates would breathe in the fog's murk and heaviness. How would they live their day-to-day lives with this thick cloud hovering above them?

"Is it only kids who have this much fear surrounding them?"

The boy shook his head and snapped again. In a blink, Theo was standing in New York's Time Square with the giant light-up screens all around him. The fog was there too. It encircled him and flowed throughout the city. He could see people walking through the fog, skin pale and with dark circles under their eyes. They all looked liked zombies going about their normal lives.

"Almost everyone lives in the darkness of fear, blinded to the light."

The boy pointed toward the sky. Theo looked up to see a river of light flowing above them. He reached up, just tall enough to wiggle his fingertips inside the warm light. A buzz spread from his fingers and rushed through his entire body. Where there was light, there was no darkness, no fear.

"Do you know what the light is, Theo?"

Theo looked at the boy with a smile stretched across his face. "The Kingdom of Heaven, right? Love!"

"Exactly." The boy snapped his fingers again.

Just like that, Theo was standing in his own living

room, looking at his dad, who sat on the couch. The thick black fog was all around him, flowing through him—so much fear.

"Dad?" Theo said and walked closer to him.

Before Theo could reach his dad, the boy snapped his fingers again. They were back on the hillside, but now the entire hill was smothered by the same thick fog of fear. And there was something else. A large, golden hot air balloon with a wicker basket sat in the middle of it all.

Theo had never actually seen a hot air balloon up close, but he knew how they worked.

"I want to show you your own fears," the boy said. "Take a closer look at the balloon."

Ignoring the drifting around them, Theo walked up to the balloon and brushed his fingers across the basket, feeling the grooves between the woven wicker. He leaned in and stared up inside the massive balloon. A gas-fed flame burned, heating the trapped air, making it less dense so that the balloon would rise.

But the balloon wasn't rising. Something was weighing it down. Theo peered over the edge to see heavy sandbags tied to the balloon. Only these sandbags were filled with more than sand. Swirling black fog seeped in and through the canvas bags, holding them in place on the shadowed grass.

"How can fog be so heavy?" Theo asked.

"Oh, it's much heavier than it looks," the boy said, climbing into the balloon. "The only way to rise above the fog is to surrender."

"Surrender?"

"You have to let go of your fear. Join me."

Theo stepped into the balloon with the boy.

"Each rope is tied to a deep fear," the boy said. "What are you afraid of, Theo?"

Theo peered over the basket again at the first sandbag and touched the rope holding it secure. "I'm afraid of not being good enough."

With his words, the rope became taut, as if he'd added even more weight to the sandbag it was tied to.

"What else?" the boy asked.

"I'm afraid of losing my dad. I'm afraid of no one liking me."

Two more ropes tightened.

"Good. What else?"

"I'm afraid that everyone is angry at me. I'm afraid that I'll never be strong enough. I'm afraid of disappointing you."

Theo's chest felt as if it had tightened with each rope, heavy as the sandbags below.

"What if you let all those fears go?" the boy asked, pulling a small dagger from his waistband. He placed it in Theo's hand. "What would happen if you cut the ropes of fear that hold you down?"

Theo stared into the boy's kind eyes and thought about his question. If he let go of his fears? He'd rise above them.

"Try it," the boy said. "Cut a rope."

"Just cut a rope?"

"Just cut a rope."

Theo walked over to the first rope, took a deep breath, and then slashed through the fibers, cutting it clean through. The balloon lifted slightly. Theo felt a bit of the pressure lift from his chest. Incredible!

"You see? Cut another one. Cut them all."

Excited now, Theo began to cut each rope that tied him down. The ropes started to snap all around him, and the balloon began to rise higher and higher off the ground.

But they were still in the fog.

The boy nodded toward the last rope. "The last one is the fear and judgment of yourself. Love the way I love: without judging."

With a swift motion, Theo slashed at the last rope. The blade cut it free with a twang and the balloon surged up through the fog and into clean air, flowing with brilliant, colorful light.

He gasped, free of the weight that had tightened his chest. The fog below was thinning quickly, and then it was gone. The whole town gleamed bright with color. The grass shown a vibrant green, and the brightly painted houses sparkled like jewels.

The fear was gone! All of it!

His right shoulder began to feel warm. He lifted his sleeve and stared at his glowing tattoo.

The red cross glowed in the middle of the green circle.

The fourth seal!

Theo rubbed his thumb across the red cross.

"Red," he said, looking over at the boy. "Surrender is the way to see the light."

The boy smiled.

"Surrender my fears. Surrender the lies that hold me in fear!"

"Yes!" the boy laughed. "Yes, now you see."

Theo spun back to the stunning view of the world he lived in far below them. "I know what I have to do now. I know what I have to do in the other world."

"You are the light of the world, Theo," the boy said. Then he snapped again.

Theo immediately found himself inside his tree house. The boy was gone, but Elyon was still there.

Theo pulled up his sleeve to make sure the fourth seal was actually real. He jumped to his feet, scrambled down the ladder, and ran back to the house. When he opened the door, he found Danny and his dad sitting at the kitchen bar, eating waffles.

His dad cocked an eyebrow. "You feeling better, buddy?"

"Much! Sorry about that. Fresh air always helps, you know, to find another seal."

Had he really just told his dad he'd gone outside to find a seal?

Danny hopped up, sending his chair scooting back. "You found it?"

"A seal?" his dad asked, confused.

"It's part of a . . . a game," Danny said.

Theo ran to his father and hugged him. "I love you, Dad. I really do."

"I love you too," his dad said, returning the embrace.

Theo removed his grip on his dad and grabbed Danny's arm. "Let's go upstairs! I know what to do."

"You boys have fun!" his dad called after them.

Theo waited for Danny to enter the room and then shut the door behind them.

"You found the fourth seal?" Danny asked, excited. "How? When? What is it?"

Theo took Danny's hand and pressed it against the seal. Danny's jaw fell open.

"Surrender," Danny whispered. "It's . . . beautiful!"

Beautiful was exactly how Theo would describe it and everything else that was the mystery of Elyon.

A warm light began to glow from under Danny's shirt as the fourth seal branded his shoulder. He grabbed his arm, feeling the heat.

"It's there?" he asked.

Theo lifted his sleeve. The first four seals glowed on Danny's shoulder—white, then green, then black, and finally the red cross.

"Yup, they're there!"

"So, what now?"

"We go back." Theo grabbed the vials of green lake water from his nightstand and placed one into Danny's hands. "I know exactly what to do."

Theo stared at the night sky of other earth. He inhaled the cool air, knowing what he had to do. And with that knowing, even though he had the fourth seal, he felt a twinge of fear—maybe more than a twinge, which was strange, because the fourth seal was surrendering his fear. So why did he feel it? Maybe he needed all five seals before they fully worked. Isn't that what Talya said? Something about more power than he could imagine with the fifth seal.

Theo sat up to find two large green eyes focused on him.

"You did it!" Stokes said. "You have the fourth seal, which means you don't need me to guide you anymore. Talya told me that it's very important for you to find the last seal on your own."

"You're leaving?" Danny asked, jerking up.

"Not that I want to, you understand." Stokes smiled at him and then looked back at Theo. "But the fifth seal is the most important and Talya was very clear."

Theo pushed himself to his feet and wrapped him up in a hug. "You're my best friend, and I never could have found any of the seals without your help."

Danny joined them in the hug. "You're the best, Stokes."

Stokes wrapped his wings around both of them and hugged them tight. "You are wise and strong now. Go do what you have to do."

Stokes stepped back, took a little bow, and then lifted into the sky. Soon the fluffy Roush was gone from sight, leaving Theo and Danny staring up into the night sky.

"Well?" Danny asked. "You said you know what we have to do."

"We have to go back into the lair. I need to find Asher."

"Not Annelee? You're sure about that? I think it would be smarter to try to get Annelee out first."

Theo bit his lip and shook his head. "I have to find Asher and talk to him first. Then we worry about Annelee."

Danny eyed him with some doubt but then offered a short nod. "Talk to him? I'm not so sure he'll agree to that, but if you say so."

"I do. Let's go."

Danny followed Theo as they retraced their steps to Shadow Man's lair. They quickly found the crack that Stokes had shown them and slipped back into the darkness that lay on the other side. Creeping down the same path they'd taken before, they reached the large cavern where Annelee lay asleep on the bed-like platform.

"He's gone," Danny whispered.

Theo scanned the walls. "So are the Shataiki."

"We could slip down there and shake her—"

"No, Asher first," Theo interrupted. "They aren't dumb enough to leave her unguarded anyway. You keep an eye on Annelee. I'll go and try to find Asher."

"You sure you can do this on your own? Asher is weirdly powerful here."

"I'll be fine. Don't do anything while I'm away."

Theo quickly crawled down the ledge to the floor of the cavern and crept to what looked like the main tunnel leading from the cave. The air was thick and cold, and he could feel the goose bumps lining his arms. He didn't know where he was going or exactly what he would do when he found Asher; he only knew that he had to deal with the bully if he wanted to save Annelee.

Finding the fifth seal was all about following what he'd learned in the first four seals. He was the light, but only by releasing his fear could he see himself as that light. And Asher was his greatest fear.

Surrendering his fear was the Kingdom glasses that would allow him to see the world in that light. As long as he feared Asher, he would be blind to that light, blind to who he really was as the light.

Rounding a wide sweeping turn in the tunnel, Theo heard the faint sound of crying. The sound was so strange in that dark place that he stopped in his tracks, mesmerized.

Theo held his breath. The sound was coming from a tunnel to his left. He headed into the passage, walking on tiptoes, curious.

As he neared the sound, Theo pressed his body against one of the walls and crept closer. The whimpering grew louder.

He crept forward and poked his head around the corner.

A lone torch flickered down the hall. There on the dirty ground he saw Asher balled against the wall, quietly weeping. Why was Asher Brox crying?

Theo stood up, took a deep breath, and stepped around the corner. "Asher?"

Asher sprang to his feet, wiping at his red eyes with the back of his hand. He looked gaunt and hollowed out, like the life had been sucked from his body. His skin was loose around his bones, and his eyes were sunken above dark circles.

"You!" Asher spat. "I hate you!"

Theo inched back a step and stared at the boy who stood before him—just a boy, mentally tortured by Shadow Man, full of anger and fear. It was hard seeing Asher so broken, even though part of him felt that the bully certainly deserved it—and more.

"I'm here to help you."

"Help me?" Asher yelled. "There's nothing wrong with me. In fact, I'm way better than my old self. Don't you see how strong I am? Shadow Man has given me unbelievable powers."

"It's all a lie." And in that moment, Theo knew it was. Fear was Asher's power, but in the light, there was no fear, so fear had to be a lie. The only thing fear could do was create more fear. Light was the truth and it healed all darkness, all fear, everything that trapped people like Asher in this terrible nightmare.

Theo realized that he wasn't afraid of Asher anymore. Instead, he felt sorry for him. What had happened to turn him into such a bully?

All Theo wanted was to get Asher out of the nightmare Shadow Man had trapped him in.

"No, Theo," Asher sneered. "It's your Elyon who lies! Shadow Man told me you'd try to poison my head with those lies."

Black smoke began to ooze from Asher's nose and eyes. The veins under his skin blackened and began to move, crawling up and down his arms. Theo took a step back, horrified by the sight. Fear. The same fear that had captured his father and that held down the hot air balloon filled Asher.

Asher grabbed his head and began to scream in pain.

"You don't have to live like this, Asher!" Theo

yelled, covering his ears. "You're light, not darkness! Elyon loves you."

Asher glared at Theo. "Loves me? No one loves me. No one! Not even my own father! Fathers are supposed to love their kids, not hit them! Now you're trying to tell me this Elyon you love so much loves me too? I'm not stupid, Theo, and I'm not falling for any more lies. There's no such thing as love!"

Theo stepped forward, struck with deep compassion for the boy. He had no idea he'd been abused, but it all made sense. Asher had never experienced real love.

"That's not true. You can live in the light. Shadow Man's the one lying to you! He's keeping you in darkness. Just look at your arms! Come with me and you can live in the light. You can be free of this."

Asher's lip began to tremble. "I can be free?"

Theo came closer, desperate for the boy to hear him now. His plan was working. "Yes. Yes, you can. All you have to do is turn to the light and surrender the fear that blinds you to it."

The sound of a chuckle echoed through the tunnels behind them.

Shadow Man was coming.

Asher began to twitch as the darkness in his veins pumped faster and faster. He crumpled over his knees and screamed at the floor. "I can never be free!" Hard sobs fell from his lips.

Theo took a step forward to comfort him. "Asher? It's going to be okay."

Asher lifted his head, eyes black. "No, it's not. I'm evil! Can't you see it?"

The Theo who started this quest would have agreed, but not now.

"You don't have to be Shadow Man's slave. He's the one who makes you think you're evil. He's fear, and he's blinded you with that fear! You can't believe his lies!"

Asher sniffed and then cocked his head and glared at Theo without expression. He slowly shook his head. An eerie smile twisted his chapped lips.

"Never," he thundered, lunging at Theo. He slashed at Theo's torso and then his face. Theo threw up his arms, trying to protect himself, but Asher's sharp nails cut deep into his skin.

Theo gasped with pain.

Cuts immediately appeared on Asher's forearms in the same places he'd cut Theo. Theo blinked, surprised by what he was seeing. Asher sliced at him again.

Theo cried out as the nails ripped at his skin just below the seals. The wound appeared on Asher's arm, deep and bleeding. But the bully didn't flinch.

"Stop!" Theo cried. "You're hurting yourself!"

Asher abruptly stopped and chuckled. "Is that so? I like pain, maggot. And so will your little troll. She'll be just like me. I'm guessing you'll love that."

Asher grabbed Theo's shoulders and threw him across the tunnel. Theo hit the wall and crumpled to the floor in pain.

"You're welcome to watch, maggot. We all go down in the end."

Asher headed back the direction Theo had come, back to where Annelee waited on the bed at the core of Shadow Man's lair.

Theo pushed himself off the floor, ignoring his pain, and struggled to hurry after Asher.

Fear had made its return, creeping through him, but he knew who he was. He was the one who knew four seals—white, black, green, and red. He could not forget! As he ran, he repeated what he had learned over and over in his head.

I am the light, and the light does not fear the dark. I am the son of Elyon. Elyon cannot be threatened. Surrender is the way to see the light.

He slowed at the cavern's entrance to catch his breath and calculate his next move. But before he could think, he heard Danny yelling like a mad man.

"Annelee!" Danny screamed, running for the center where Asher had reached Annelee.

Danny was frantic, and Theo could see why.

Asher leaned over her, holding her arms down as she struggled weakly. Theo joined in with Danny, both sprinting toward the center platform.

"Annelee!"

But Annelee didn't respond. As Theo drew near, he could see her eyes wide in dread and her exposed arm where the symbols should have been.

"Get away from her, you thug!" Theo roared. "Don't you dare hurt her!"

"You come any closer, and I'll break her neck," Asher snapped.

Danny skidded to a stop. Theo slowed, limping up to Danny. He tried not to think about his own pain—the cuts, the impact with the wall. Annelee needed him.

"Asher, please, let her go," he begged. "We can help you, but you have to let us."

"Well, well, well, what do we have here?" a low voice chuckled from their right.

Theo twisted to see Shadow Man emerging from a dark corner of the cavern.

"Having fun without me, Asher?" He walked to the platform. "Now, now, don't hurt the poor girl . . . yet. We need a second soul to join you."

Shadow Man turned his head toward Theo. "Ready to finish my game, son of Elyon?"

"**H**ere is how the game is going to end," Shadow Man said, glaring down at Theo. "First . . ." He snapped his fingers.

Two large Shataiki swooped down from the shadows high above. They landed behind Danny and had his arms in their claws before he could avoid them. He struggled with a cry, but it was no use. The more he struggled, the deeper their claws cut into his flesh. He went limp, trembling in fear.

Shadow Man strolled toward Theo. "Good. Now bring the girl to me, Asher."

Asher jerked Annelee off the bed, wrenched her arms behind her back, and shoved her forward, holding her wrists tight. Theo watched, helpless and unnerved by the empty stare on Annelee's face. She was confused and lost.

"Stay put!" Asher snarled, pulling her to a stop in front of Shadow Man.

"Yes, stay put, sweetheart," Shadow Man said, flashing his wicked grin. "It seems that this ugly little thing apparently means a lot to you, so here is what's going to happen." Shadow Man grabbed Annelee by her shoulder and shoved Asher to the ground like a forgotten toy.

He shifted his eyes to Theo. "You're going to take her place. You'll surrender your seals and agree to play her part in our game between the worlds. If you don't, I'll let Asher break both your necks like he so desires to do."

"No, Theo!" Danny yelled.

Theo's mind spun. Surrender the seals? He could never do that! And he could never join Asher in bringing destruction to the other world. He looked at Annelee.

"You need her to cross into my world," Theo said.

"Do I? I can already bridge the worlds, you fool. Didn't you see my Shataiki? Two would create a portal in both worlds, but I'm willing to work with one. Two just makes it a whole lot easier. The choice is yours. Surrender the seals or surrender Annelee."

"I can't surrender the seals!"

"Why? Because you'd forget who you are? Nearly

all those in your world have forgotten who they are. Most have never known who they are. They're lost in a state of blindness, and they don't even know it. Would it be so bad to be like everyone else? You'd fit right in. You'd be one of them—none the wiser. It's a small price to pay for the girl you love, wouldn't you say?"

Annelee stared at him dumbly. Shadow Man was speaking at least some truth. Not having the seals would make him like everyone in his world—lost in the fog of fear. He'd forget Elyon and the truths he'd discovered. He'd be just like his dad and most everyone else he knew. Would that be so bad?

Then again, his mission was to find all five seals. Could he really give up the first four now?

"Make your decision," Shadow Man snapped. He shoved Annelee to the ground. She collapsed in a heap in front of Theo.

He dropped to the floor and helped her to her knees. Her frightened eyes stared into his, and in that moment, he knew he could never let any harm come to her.

He'd known from the moment he'd cut the last sand bag with the boy that he would surrender his greatest fear. He knew it now as clearly as he knew the other four seals. His greatest fear wasn't Asher. It was death.

Giving up the seals would be like dying. He'd give up knowing who he truly was. He'd be dead, another zombie waking through the halls of school.

But he would do it to save her.

Theo brushed the hair from her face and placed his hand on her shoulder to get her attention. "Remember who you are," he whispered. "You're the daughter of the King. You're the light of the world. Never forget."

Hopefully, Annelee would find a way to keep him from destroying their world.

"None of your silly talk means anything here, you fool!" Shadow Man snarled. "Surrender the seals or Asher takes her head!"

"I give you my seals, Annelee. I surrender them all and place them as a seal on your arm."

His arm grew hot. Light flowed from his sleeve. He reached out to her shoulder and sealed her with an intense heat that made her gasp.

In that one long drawn-out moment, it was like someone had pulled the plug from Theo's life. All of his strength drained, leaving him weak. His head filled with a haze of confusion and his chest tightened with fear.

And then he was falling to the floor.

"Theo?" Annelee rushed forward, weeping. "No, no, no! Take them back!"

He was too weak to respond. She had the seals. They were important, but he couldn't remember why they were important.

Shadow Man snapped his fingers, and two Shataiki swooped in to haul Annelee away from Theo as she screamed, weeping over him.

Shadow Man chuckled. "Thank you, boy. From the beginning, this whole game was yours—every moment, every encounter. I nearly had you with Ruza and then with the Horde girl. But now . . . oh, but now! The key was always you, the strong one, but I knew you would stumble. They always do. And to top it off, now I have two little slaves." He winked at Annelee and Danny who were both in the clutches of his minions. "And soon I'll have four."

"Receive my fear, Theo." Shadow Man breathed in Theo's direction, and with that breath, tendrils of fog spilled from his lips, seeking out their new host.

Theo tried to focus, but he couldn't think straight. His body was heavy. Numb. The black fog reached him, slithering into his eyes, nose, and mouth.

A deep fear, burning like fire, edged into his bones and veins. He was dying! But he didn't want to die. So he screamed, grabbing at the fog, flailing his arms, desperate to be free of the fear.

But his screaming only made it easier for the black fog to flow into his mouth.

And then Theo knew only fear.

He collapsed, numb to the world.

Somewhere in the outer world, Shadow Man was chuckling. Shataiki were shrieking. A girl was weeping. A blind boy was screaming his name.

None of it mattered. He was dead. And if he wasn't, he wanted to be.

Theo.

He heard a voice so close that it might have been his own breath.

Theo. Remember who you are.

Who am I? he thought.

I love you, Theo, and there is no fear in love.

He hesitated as the rest of the world faded from his consciousness. His friends were out there, calling for him. But they were like distant abstractions to him now.

He was talking to a voice—a voice inside of him.

Let my love heal you, Theo.

Theo lifted one hand and rested it on his chest, groaning. "There is no love."

The voice giggled. He was sure he recognized that giggle.

Of course there is! It's the light, remember? I showed it to you. Do you want to see it again?

Could he trust that voice?

"Where is the light?" he asked himself. "I only see darkness."

I am the light. You are the light, made in my likeness, the light of the world.

"I'm the light?"

The boy giggled again, totally free of concern or fear. It was so freeing that Theo found himself shutting out everything but the sound of the boy giggling, in spite of all the fear and darkness that pressed down on him. Who could be so powerful that they would smile in the face of such fear and death?

Then Theo remembered something.

"Elyon," he whispered.

Hello, Theo. Open your eyes.

Theo opened his eyes to find himself submerged in water and surrounded by a light so bright that he thought it might blind him. Elyon?

The giggle echoed all around him. Theo's fear fell away, replaced by a deep wonder and knowing. It *was* Elyon! The boy! Theo had been here before. He was in the lake of water he could breathe.

Theo took a deep breath and allowed the light to wash through him. Beauty and love seeped into every nerve, every muscle, every bone.

The water began to swirl, forming a vortex around him. Then he was moving up, up, at a high rate of speed. Within seconds, Theo was no longer in the green water but landing on a beach of white sand.

He looked up to see that before him were two trees, one black and one white. Between them were the boy and his lion: Elyon and Judah.

The boy smiled at him. "Welcome back."

Theo stood, dumbstruck.

"I . . ." He didn't know what to say. "Where am I?"

The boy spread his arms. "Let's call it the Garden of Eden, my paradise, my kingdom."

Theo glanced back at the water shimmering green and gold and then in front of him, beyond the white sand and beyond the two trees. A brilliant forest of green swayed in a breeze that smelled of flowers and candy. The trees were heavy with many fruits of all sizes, shapes and colors.

The Kingdom. He'd seen it before.

Theo returned his attention to the two trees on either side of the boy. The white one, filled with many white fruits, was glowing beautiful and powerful.

The black one had no leaves, only sharp razor-like branches. Small plum-sized fruits, each part-black and part-white, drooped from the limbs.

"You're wondering about the trees," the boy said.

Theo faced him. "What are they?"

"The white tree is called the Tree of Life. It is light and love, which is true life."

"So the Tree of Love?"

"Sure."

"And that one?" Theo pointed to the black tree.

"That is the Tree of the Knowledge of Good and Evil—death. It is the tree of judgment, which brings fear because you can only fear what you judge in the knowledge of good and evil."

"So the knowledge of good and evil brings fear. The Tree of Judgment or the Tree of Fear?"

"They're the same, really."

Theo looked at the small black-and-white fruits on the Tree of Judgment. Black and white. The knowledge of good and evil. Judgment that brings fear.

The boy plucked a fruit from the white tree and handed it to Theo. "Try it."

Theo accepted the white fruit and took a big bite. Warmth and wonder filled him as soon as the sweet juice flooded his mouth. He took another bite, unable to stifle his laughter.

"Good?" the boy asked, smiling.

"Delicious!"

The boy stepped over to the Tree of Judgment and plucked a fruit. He handed it to Theo

"Now, try this one."

Theo hesitated but took the black-and-white fruit, examining it closer.

The knowledge of good and evil. Judgment. "I should eat it?"

"It's okay," the boy said. "I'm right here."

Theo bit into the fruit. As if someone had stuck an electric cord into his mouth, his body jerked. The juice was bitter, like bile, but worse. Terrible anger and fear of darkness swallowed him. It was like death, like Shadow Man's fog.

He cried out, dropped the fruit, and then shoved the other fruit—the white one that tasted so sweet—into his mouth. The fear immediately fell away. Theo took another bite, lost again in the wonder of it all.

"Do you know what you're tasting?" the boy asked.

Theo knew. "Love."

The boy nodded. "Life that is light and love. You're the light of the world, but you don't always experience that light because planks of judgment block your sight of it."

"Can I make the planks go away?"

"When you're seeing the light, you'll always experience love. That's how you know. Love is the evidence of being in the light. So when you experience fear, you haven't surrendered judgment."

"The seals! The fourth seal was surrender. When I surrender my fears, I surrender judgment." He could see the light, the light he could only experience as love.

"Now you're getting it!" the boy said. "It's simple, right?"

"Simple," Theo said, and took another bite of the white fruit.

"Taste and see that I am good," the boy said.

"Delicious!" Theo cried around a mouthful

of the sweet juice. He thrust his hand into the air. "Amazing!"

"Love is more than amazing," the boy laughed. "There is no fear in love. Love holds no record of wrong. Love is life itself! Everything else is fear and death."

"Forget death. I want life!" He knew he was being silly, but in that moment, silliness seemed totally appropriate. He didn't have a care in the world.

"So do I." The boy walked up to Theo and placed a hand on his shoulder. "So tell me, Theo, which fruit will you live your life by?"

"Love," he said. His eyes went wide. "That's the fifth seal, isn't it?"

The boy winked.

"Love is the evidence of being in the light." Theo's right shoulder grew hot and began to glow bright as the seals returned—not only the first four, but the final seal as well.

A white circle appeared in the middle of the red cross, like a pin holding all five seals together.

White: Elyon is the light without darkness. Green: I am the light. Black: My journey is to see the light in darkness. Red: Surrender is the means of seeing the light. White: Love is the evidence of being in the light.

Theo's heart was so full that he thought it might burst. His mind went to Annelee and Danny, the friends whom he loved dearly. Then he thought of Talya and Justin, his leaders who had left breadcrumbs for him to follow.

He thought of his Roush, his guides and protectors—Michal, Gabil and Stokes—how he loved them dearly. Finally, he thought of Asher, whom he'd once hated so deeply.

But now all he wanted to do was show Asher how truly loved he was.

"Do you remember the teaching of Jesus on the hill?" the boy asked. "He stood in front of a huge crowd and told them all that they were the light of the world but that they'd hidden that light under a basket—another identity called the world. They'd forgotten who they were. When you are in love, you can see the light in others, just like Jesus."

"So I can love Asher as the light."

"You cannot be in the light and hold another in darkness. And now, I see that you are ready. When the time comes, I'll give you the words. Close your eyes, Theo."

He closed his eyes and took a deep breath.

Now open your eyes and see, the voice whispered inside of him.

When Theo opened his eyes, Shadow Man was standing where he had been before, as if only a second had passed. The man was gloating, until he looked at Theo's bright eyes. His face went from delight to fear—and then fury.

His eyes shifted to the five glowing seals on Theo's arm. He shoved a trembling finger in Theo's face. "Kill him, Asher! Kill him now!"

Life surged through Theo so vibrantly and powerfully that fear seemed like a distant dream. There was no fear in love because fear didn't exist in the space of love. And he was experiencing that love.

The cavern seemed to be moving in slow motion around him. Annelee and Danny cried out Theo's name as four Shataiki held them back.

Shadow Man stood stock-still, face twisted with wrath.

Asher lumbered toward Theo with black eyes and bloodstained clothes. Judgment had blinded him to the light, including the light that was in him. Wasn't it that way with most people when pushed to the limit?

Theo felt nothing but love for Asher now. The bully in Asher had only been replicating what he'd been taught by his father. All Asher had ever done to Theo was a faint memory that no longer held him in fear.

Asher dove at Theo. He wrapped his fingers around Theo's throat.

Theo didn't flinch. He locked his eyes with Asher's.

"You are the light of the world," Theo said calmly.

Asher tightened his grip, but then his eyes momentarily widened, as if something had interrupted his rage.

"Don't listen to his lies, you little puke!" Shadow Man marched toward them. "Kill him!"

Theo lifted his hand, placed it on Asher's cheek, and looked deep into his eyes. "Asher, I love you. You are far more powerful and beautiful than you can possibly know." Beautiful—the word he had used to describe the mysteries of Elyon. "The boy showed me. You're not who your father tells you that you are. You're loved. You *are* love."

Ripples of light seeped from Theo's hand, overpowering Asher's ability to breathe until he finally gasped.

Stunned, Asher released Theo and backed away. Tears slipped from his eyes. He collapsed to his knees as the light joined with the light inside of Asher, cleansing him from the darkness that had blinded him.

"No!" Shadow Man snarled, trembling.

When the time comes, I'll give you the words.

He knew what to say. Seeing his advantage, Theo spun to Annelee and Danny. "Love! It's the fifth seal. Love Asher. Love is the light that ends the darkness. You can't sweep a shadow from a room. You only have to turn the light on." He thrust a hand at Shadow Man. "He's a shadow!"

Annelee twisted and faced Asher. "I love you, Asher." Tears streamed down her face. "I'm so sorry for everything. I love you."

Danny was joining in, but all Theo heard was the sudden roar of light that rushed into the lair. It reached Asher and swirled around him like a tornado.

Shadow Man was backing away, terrified.

The thousands of Shataiki hidden in the far reaches of the great hall began to hiss and shriek, fleeing for the tunnels, desperate to be gone from the light.

Asher's eyes were no longer black but a vibrant blue. He knelt there shaking, sucking in the light as if he were breathing for the first time. Tears of gratitude washed his cheeks as love consumed him.

Shadow Man cowered against the cavern wall.

The words continued to flow from Theo. "There

is no darkness in light. There is no fear in love. Death is only a shadow."

A burst of light erupted all around them. And as with any shadow, Shadow Man vanished in that light. For a moment the light grew until it was so bright that Theo couldn't see anything but white.

With a sudden *whoosh*, it collapsed back in on itself, taking the lair with it. It was gone, simply gone.

In its place the four travelers from another world found themselves in a lush green garden. Birds were chirping and the breeze was blowing. The sun was rising on the eastern horizon, casting long rays over a blue lake to their right.

Asher was still on his knees, mouth agape. Annelee and Danny stood side by side, gawking.

It was Annelee who found her voice first. "Is . . . is this the Kingdom of Heaven?"

"Beautiful, isn't it?" Talya said from behind her.

Annelee turned to his voice and ran up to him, laughing in delight. She threw her arms around him and buried her cheek in his stomach.

"There, there. Now, now. I'm an old man, no need to break me." He laughed and returned her hug.

His eyes quickly found Asher, who was too taken aback to speak. He walked toward the boy, eyebrow arched.

"I see you can finally see who you are," the old man said.

Asher glanced at Theo and then at Talya. "I'm the light of the world, a child of Elyon."

Talya ruffled his hair with a big hand. "That you are," he chuckled. "That you are."

Theo knelt on one knee beside Asher and put his arm around his shoulder. "That you are."

Asher laughed in abandon. Theo had never heard him laugh like this. He joined in. It was as if two friends had reunited after a long absence. Annelee and Danny joined the huddle on the ground, hugging their new friend.

Theo released Asher and quickly rolled up his sleeve, revealing all five seals: white, green, black, red, and white. Danny and Annelee took turns as they touched the last seal and received its knowledge.

Theo looked up at Asher. "Would you like to know the truth?"

"Please," Asher breathed.

"Put your hand on my shoulder."

Asher willingly placed his hand on Theo's seals.

Each seal began to appear on Asher's shoulder. Theo knew that Asher understood as the truth washed over him.

"Amazing," Asher whispered. "I don't know how else to describe it."

"We can't!" Theo knew exactly what Asher was talking about. "I'm not sure love can be described. It can only be experienced."

Talya lifted a hand. "If you're all quite done, I have one last thing for you to do before you return. Please, follow me."

The four followed in silence, taking in the lush landscape of trees and flowers. Birds chirped and the leaves above them rustled in the breeze, but another distant sound had joined in nature's chorus.

It was a sound like cheering.

They rounded a bend and found themselves at the entrance to a massive amphitheater carved into the side of a mountain. Inside sat thousands of fluffy white Roush, lining hundreds of rows, all staring at them and cheering.

A smile split Theo's face as he gazed around the amphitheater. There was a stage at the center, and on that stage waited his three friends—Michal, Gabil, and, of course, his fluffy best friend, Stokes. Next to them stood Justin, the one he knew in his world as Jesus, and the lion, Judah.

Only then did it occur to Theo that this moment was meant for him, Annelee, Danny, and Asher. Everyone had gathered because Theo had succeeded in his quest.

Theo ran down the steps of the amphitheater, followed by his friends, and took to the stage, where he tackled the three Roush. They rolled and wrestled as they had once done before. The Roush watching cheered them on.

"Theo, son of Dunnery," Justin said. A hush fell over the Roush. Theo jumped to his feet and stood strong next to Justin as he spoke.

"Tell us all what you've learned."

"I have found the five Seals of Truth. And I experienced the truth of Elyon, myself, and the world we live in."

"Tell us, son of Elyon, what are these five Seals of Truth?"

Theo took a deep breath and loudly proclaimed, "White: Elyon is the light of the world without darkness."

As one, the whole gathering repeated the first seal.

"Green: I am the light!"

Again, a thunderous roar echoed the seal back to him.

"Black: Our journey is to see the light in darkness."

"Black: Our journey is to see the light in darkness," echoed the Roush and those on the stage.

"Red: Surrender is the means of seeing the light."

Theo grabbed Asher's hand as the Roush repeated the fourth seal.

Theo lifted a fist in the air. "White: Love is the evidence of being in the light."

A great cheer broke out after they repeated the final seal. It was the capstone, the seal that revealed the full truth of the other four seals.

Talya approached them from the side. "Well done, my friends." His eyes shifted to Theo. "You have completed your quest, and you have done so with grace and maturity beyond your years. Take the lessons you've learned here and apply them to your lives in that world. Show the others in your school the love you know and understand. Consider it your new quest. Agreed?"

"Agreed!" they said in unison.

"Now you are ready to go home," Talya said.

Theo wondered if he would ever return to other earth. He would miss the friends he'd made and the adventures that each quest had brought them.

He smiled at his three fluffy, green-eyed guides. Each of them returned the smile as a final goodbye.

"Don't worry, Theo," Stokes said. "We will see you again. Promise."

Theo rushed over and gave Stokes a big hug. "I'll miss you, Shataiki Slayer."

"I'll miss you too, mighty warrior."

He would have hugged the others as well, but Talya cleared his throat. "Ready?"

Theo took a last look around. "I'm ready."

One by one, Talya touched their foreheads, and then Theo was waking up in another world.

It had been two days since Theo had seen the others. Danny had woken up with him in his room, but Annelee and Asher had woken up in their own homes, where they'd fallen asleep.

His dad had quickly noticed a difference in him the next day. "What's happened to you, Theo?"

"What do you mean?"

"I mean, you seem so confident and full of life! Not that you haven't been, but you seem so . . . I don't know. Alive!"

Theo had smiled. "I'm seeing the world differently, that's all. I guess I'm learning to love life."

He would share more with his dad as time passed, but he didn't want to spill it all at once. He had a lot to process. And he wasn't sure how his dad would react to tales of his quest for the five seals in other earth. Eventually, his dad would understand and learn himself. At least, that's what Theo hoped.

"You sure everything's okay, Theo?" his dad asked as he pulled the car into their usual spot at the school Monday morning.

"More than okay," he said. "I promise."

"You're not entering a new phase of denial are you?"

"Nope," he said. "Nothing like denial. More like truth and acceptance."

"Okay. Just checking."

Theo jumped out of the car and headed to the double doors. He was excited, eager for their reunion. They hadn't spoken all weekend. There was so much to talk about, so much to learn—mostly how having the five seals would affect their daily lives in this world.

He poked is head into Mrs. Baily's classroom. Empty. He had some time before class started, so he headed straight for the library. The secret room where he'd first found the book drew him like a moth to a flame.

He walked through the library door to find Mrs. Friend organizing books in the fiction section. She smiled, eyes bright.

"Theo! The beautiful face I've had the pleasure of

seeing in my little square of the school so often these past weeks. You look positively alive!"

"Hi, Mrs. Friend!"

"Did you find what you were looking for?" she asked with a wink.

She knew about the quests! Maybe she knew before he did. Why else would she have led him to the room with book?

"I did," he said.

She crossed her arms and studied him. "I can see that you did. Well done, brave one." She paused. "They're waiting for you."

He spun and headed for the stairs.

"Theo?" Mrs. Friend's voice followed him. He turned back. "The room is yours whenever you like. Use it wisely, yes?"

"I will!" he said, and then bounded up the stairs.

The door to the small room was already open. Theo hurried inside. There stood Asher, Annelee and Danny, arms crossed.

Annelee winked. "We've been waiting for you."

Asher stepped forward and handed Theo the leather book that had started it all: *The Book of History.* "Think this is yours," he said sheepishly.

Theo pushed the book back into Asher's hands. "The book belongs to all of us."

"It better, dream traveler," Annelee said with a laugh.

"I wouldn't mind another adventure to other earth at some point," Danny said, adjusting his dark glasses.

Asher dropped his head. "Maybe next time I can be a little more helpful."

"You were plenty helpful," Theo said. "Without you, I never would have found the fifth seal. I guess we all played our part. Speaking of which, we have a new quest—here, at school."

"They're going to freak out, seeing me with you," Asher said.

"Can't you just see their faces?" Annelee laughed.

Theo nodded. "We'll show love more than we talk about it."

Theo was overwhelmed with gratitude for each of his new friends. He couldn't wait to see what a transformed bully, the new girl who had discovered her true beauty, a boy who had learned to see with different lenses, and he, Theo Dunnery, the fearless dream traveler, could do to turn a school upside down with the power of five simple Seals of Truth.

"So, are we ready?"

Annelee, Danny, and Asher nodded.

"All right then. The world is waiting. Let's do this!"

THE END

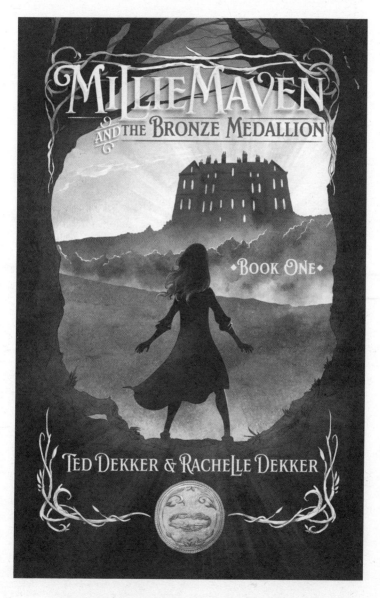